THE JUNGLE BOOK

Walt Disney's CLASSIC

THE JUNGLE BOOK

Based on Walt Disney's
full-length animated classic

Adapted by Jan Carr

SCHOLASTIC INC.
New York Toronto London Auckland Sydney

ISBN 0-590-43516-7
© The Walt Disney Company.
All rights reserved. Published by Scholastic Inc.

12 11 10 9 8 7 6 5 4 3 2   0 1 2 3 4 5/9

Printed in the U.S.A.   28

First Scholastic printing, June 1990

1

The jungles of India are wild. The trees are thickset and the brush is overgrown. Though some pockets of people clear the trees and build villages there, mostly animals live in the jungle. These are exotic animals — brightly feathered birds, darkly spotted leopards, elephants, monkeys, and tigers. The jungle is a beautiful place, but it can also be quite savage.

There are many strange legends told about the jungles of India, but none are so strange as the story of a small boy named Mowgli. His story began early one morning. A sleek black panther named Bagheera was prowling in the trees when he heard an unfamiliar sound. Bagheera pricked up his ears. The sound was one never heard before in this dense part of the jungle. It was the sound of a baby crying.

The crying came from a battered canoe. Inside the canoe was a basket and inside the basket was a baby. Bagheera cocked his head at the strange-looking Man-cub. The little baby gurgled and smiled.

Bagheera started to turn away. He didn't know how to take care of a baby. But he knew that if he left the Man-cub abandoned in the canoe, it would die. He thought of taking the Man-cub to the nearest Man-village, but that was many days' journey, and he knew that the Man-cub would need food and a mother's care right away. Then Bagheera remembered a family of wolves that lived nearby. The mother wolf had just given birth to a litter of cubs. Perhaps she could care for one more, Bagheera thought.

Bagheera grabbed the rim of the basket between his teeth and carried it to the cave where the wolves lived. He set the basket down at the cave's mouth and gave it a gentle nudge. The Man-cub was startled and began to cry. Bagheera ran behind the bushes to watch what would happen.

Just as he suspected, the wolves heard the Man-cub's cries and were curious. First, the little wolf cubs poked their heads out of the cave. They gathered around the crying bundle and poked their snouts at it, trying to figure out what it was. Then the mother wolf nudged her way through her cubs. When she saw the baby, she smiled. Behind the bushes, Bagheera sighed in relief.

But behind the mother came Rama, the father wolf. Bagheera knew that Rama would not be so easily charmed. Rama scowled at the baby. The baby stared at Rama. Suddenly the tiny infant stopped crying and began to gurgle happily. Rama's scowl melted into a smile. He, too, had been won over.

As Bagheera watched, the mother wolf picked up the basket and carried it into the cave. Rama and her cubs followed close behind. Mowgli had been adopted. He had been accepted into a loving wolf family.

2

Years passed. Ten times the rains came and went. Bagheera continued to stop by the wolf cave to see how Mowgli was doing. The boy had grown tall. He now ran with the wolf cubs. He could howl, just as they did. And all the wolf cubs loved him.

Bagheera was glad to see how well Mowgli was faring, but he knew that, someday, the boy would have to return to his own kind.

One night, the elders of the wolf pack held a meeting at Council Rock. They were worried about Mowgli. Shere Khan, a fierce tiger, had just returned to their part of the jungle. Akela, the leader of the wolves, spoke to all the others.

"Shere Khan will surely kill the boy, and all who try to protect him," he said. "Are we all in agreement as to what must be done?"

The other wolves nodded.

"Well," said Akela, "it is my unpleasant duty

4

to tell the boy's father. Rama!" he called. "Come over here, please."

Rama joined the elders.

"The council has reached its decision," said Akela. "The Man-cub can no longer stay with the pack. He must leave at once."

"Leave?" said Rama. He was shocked at the news. "But the Man-cub is like my own son. He will never survive alone in the jungle. Surely he's entitled to the protection of the pack."

Akela was firm. "Even the strength of the pack is no match for the tiger," he said.

Bagheera had been watching the meeting from the branch of a nearby tree. He leaped off the limb and walked toward the wolves.

"Perhaps I can be of help," he said.

"You, Bagheera?" said Akela. "How?"

"I know of a Man-village where he'll be safe," said Bagheera. "Mowgli and I have taken many walks together in the jungle so I'm sure he'll go with me."

"So be it," said Akela. "Go now. There's no time to lose."

As Rama watched sadly, Bagheera went to the cave to get Mowgli.

"Good luck!" Akela called after him.

And then Bagheera, with Mowgli beside him, left the wolf pack, and the two walked off together into the thick, dark jungle.

3

They were a strange twosome, the panther and the boy. Bagheera led the way through the dark jungle, with only the moon to light the path. It was very late and Mowgli was getting tired. He hopped on his friend's back and let out a big yawn.

"Bagheera," he said, "I'm getting a little sleepy. Shouldn't we start back home?"

Bagheera had not yet told the boy where they were going. He knew that it was time to tell Mowgli the truth.

"Mowgli," he said, "this time you're not going back. I'm taking you to a Man-village."

"But why?" asked Mowgli.

"Because Shere Khan has returned to this part of the jungle," said Bagheera, "and he has sworn to kill you."

"Kill me?" said Mowgli. He slid off Bagheera's back. "But why would he want to do that?"

"Because he hates man," Bagheera explained,

"and Shere Khan is not going to allow you to grow up to become a man, just another hunter with a gun."

"Oh," said Mowgli innocently, "we'd just explain to him that I'd never do a thing like that."

Bagheera whirled to face the boy.

"Nonsense!" he said. "No one explains anything to Shere Khan!"

Mowgli swallowed hard.

"Well, maybe not," he said. "But I'm not afraid. And besides, I — "

"That's enough!" Bagheera cut Mowgli short. "We'll spend the night here. Things will look better in the morning."

Mowgli turned and looked wistfully back toward the home from which he had come.

"Man-cub!" Bagheera said firmly. He was standing at the base of a tree. "Now, come on. Go on up this tree. It'll be safer there. Up you go," he ordered.

Mowgli looked up at the tree. He was used to sleeping in a cave. The tree looked awfully tall.

"That limb way up there?" he asked.

"That's right," said Bagheera.

Mowgli grabbed hold of the tree trunk and tried to pull his way up. He slipped. He grabbed the tree trunk tighter. He slipped again.

"Can't you climb any better than that?" asked Bagheera.

"It's too big around," complained Mowgli. "And besides, I don't have claws like you do."

Bagheera got underneath the boy and pushed him up to the limb. Then he scrambled up, too. Mowgli sat moodily at the base of the limb, hugging the tree trunk.

"It's time for you to get some sleep," said Bagheera. "We've got a long journey ahead of us tomorrow."

"But I want to stay in the jungle," Mowgli whined.

"You wouldn't last one day," said Bagheera.

As far as Bagheera was concerned, the discussion was over. He was tired. He stretched out on the limb to go to sleep. His eyelids fluttered closed.

As Bagheera drifted off to sleep, a long python stuck its head out of the leaves and eyed Mowgli hungrily. Mowgli didn't notice the snake. He was looking out into the dark night.

"I'm not afraid," he said. "I can look out for myself."

4

The snake dropped down in front of Mowgli and looked the boy up and down.

"S-s-say, what have we here?" hissed the snake. "It's-s-s a Man-cub. A delicious-s-s Man-cub!"

Mowgli wasn't at all afraid. He just pushed the python away.

"Go away," he said. "Leave me alone."

Across the branch, Bagheera stirred. He thought Mowgli was talking to him.

"Leave you alone," he muttered sleepily, "that's exactly what I should do. But I won't. Now, go to sleep."

"Yes, go to sleep, Man-cub," hissed the snake.

The snake looked Mowgli directly in the eye. As he did, Mowgli's eyes glazed over. The boy began to sway drowsily. The python was charming him! He was putting Mowgli into a trance!

"Sleep, little Man-cub," said the snake hypnotically. "Sleep. Sleep."

Mowgli's eyelids began to flutter shut. The python wrapped his tail around the boy and pulled it tight.

"Ba-Ba-Ba-Bagheera." Mowgli tried to call for help, but his voice was weak and sleepy.

"Quiet," mumbled Bagheera. "No more talk until morning."

"Ha ha!" the snake laughed. "The Man-cub won't be here in the morning!"

Then the snake opened his mouth wide. He was going to swallow Mowgli whole!

That voice! Bagheera was startled awake. He opened his eyes and saw little Mowgli wrapped in the python's coils. Bagheera recognized the snake right away. It was Kaa, a very dangerous jungle character who could hypnotize anyone just by staring into his eyes. Bagheera leaped to his feet to save Mowgli.

"Hold it, Kaa!" he cried.

Bagheera clobbered Kaa on the head. Mowgli wriggled free. Kaa shook his head in pain and glared at Bagheera.

"You have just made a serious mistake," Kaa said angrily. "A very stupid mistake."

Kaa slithered toward Bagheera. "Look me in the eye when I'm speaking to you," he ordered. "Both eyes!"

Bagheera yawned. The python was hypnotizing him, too! Mowgli snuck up behind Kaa and pushed at his coils.

"Aaaagh!" cried Kaa. He fell out of the tree and landed in a crumpled heap at its base.

"Just you wait till I get you in my coils!" he called up angrily. Kaa tried to slither away, but his tail caught on the tree. He yanked it loose and slid off into the jungle.

Mowgli shook Bagheera.

"Wake up," he said.

Bagheera blinked his eyes groggily. He was angry at Mowgli.

"So, you can look out for yourself, can you?" he said. "So you want to stay in the jungle, do you?"

"Yes," said Mowgli. He crossed his arms stubbornly against his chest. "I want to stay in the jungle."

Bagheera sighed. "For the last time, go to sleep!" he said.

Bagheera settled back down on the branch. It had been a long, tiring night. Soon Bagheera was asleep and snoring. But not Mowgli. Mowgli leaned against the tree and listened to the night sounds of the jungle.

5

Early the next morning, the sun rose on Bagheera and Mowgli sleeping in the tree. Mowgli had finally fallen asleep and was cuddled up in Bagheera's soft fur.

"Hup, two, three, four!" sounded a voice. It echoed through the quiet jungle, disturbing the morning peace.

Mowgli opened his eyes and blinked.

"Keep it up, two, three, four!" the voice came again.

It was a herd of elephants, marching through the clearing. They were marching in a straight line, each one's trunk holding the next one's tail.

"A parade!" cried Mowgli.

Bagheera covered his eyes with his paws.

"Oh, no," he moaned. "It's the Dawn Patrol."

Mowgli swung down to the ground and ran to investigate. At the head of the line was the elephant who was shouting commands. That was Colonel Hathi, and he was the elephant in charge. At the rear of the line was a little baby elephant.

Mowgli grinned and ran to catch up with him.

"Hello!" said Mowgli brightly. "What are you doing?"

"Shhh!" said the baby elephant. "We're drilling."

"Can I do it, too?" asked Mowgli.

"Sure," said the baby elephant. "Just do what I do. But don't talk in the ranks. It's against regulations."

Mowgli fell in line behind the baby elephant. He tried to imitate the way the elephants were marching. He swung his arms in time to their step.

"To the rear, march!" called Colonel Hathi.

At that, all the elephants turned on their heels and marched in the other direction. Now Mowgli was at the front of the line!

"Company, halt!" called Colonel Hathi. Mowgli kept marching. He didn't know what any of the commands actually meant.

" 'Halt' means 'stop'!" whispered the baby.

"Inspection!" called Colonel Hathi.

The elephants fell into line and stood at attention. They raised their trunks high in salute. Colonel Hathi moved down the line, inspecting each one. Mowgli stood next to the baby elephant and stuck his nose out as far as he could, imitating the way the elephants stuck out their trunks.

"Like this?" he said.

"That's right," said the baby elephant.

Colonel Hathi was moving toward them.

"Oh, there you are," Colonel Hathi said to the baby. The tone of his voice turned less stern, more affectionate. "Ha ha, keep those heels together, shall we, son?"

"Okay, Pop, sir," said the baby.

Colonel Hathi continued down the line and stopped in front of Mowgli.

"Well, a new recruit," he said. Then he took a closer look. "I say, what happened to your trunk? Hah!" he cried. "A Man-cub! This is treason! Sabotage! I'll have no Man-cub in my jungle!"

The Colonel picked Mowgli up in his trunk. Mowgli squirmed to get free.

"It's not your jungle," said Mowgli angrily. He hauled off and kicked Colonel Hathi in the shins.

"Hold it! Hold it!" cried Bagheera. He leaped out of the tree to help. "I can explain everything," he said to Colonel Hathi. "The Man-cub is with me. I'm taking him to the Man-village."

"To stay?" asked Colonel Hathi sternly.

"You have the word of Bagheera," the panther said gravely.

"Good," said Colonel Hathi. He turned to his troops. "Well, let's get on with it. Forward, march!" he cried.

"Come on," Bagheera whispered to Mowgli. "Let's get out of here. Quick, before anything else happens."

6

Bagheera sprinted through the jungle and jumped onto a log that crossed a rushing river. Mowgli ran, trying to keep up.

"Bagheera, we're not really going to the Man-village, are we?" Mowgli called ahead to his friend.

"Yes," said Bagheera sternly. "And we're going right now!"

"No!" Mowgli stopped short at the foot of the log. "I'm not going," he said stubbornly.

"Oh, yes you are," said Bagheera.

Mowgli grabbed the trunk of a small tree and wrapped his arms around it tightly.

"I'm staying right here," he said.

"Man-cub," said Bagheera, "you're going if I have to drag you every step of the way."

Bagheera stalked over to the boy and clamped his teeth onto Mowgli's britches.

"You let go of me!" shouted Mowgli.

Bagheera pulled on the britches. Mowgli clutched the trunk with all his strength.

15

"OH!"

The britches tore in Bagheera's mouth and Bagheera fell backwards. SPLASH! He landed right in the river.

"That does it!" Bagheera said angrily. "I've had it, Man-cub! From now on, you're on your own."

Bagheera shook the water from his face. Then he turned and stalked off into the jungle, leaving Mowgli alone at the edge of the river.

"Don't worry about me!" Mowgli shouted after him. Mowgli watched Bagheera disappear into the trees. He was trying to sound brave, but, actually, he wasn't at all sure what he would do next.

Now Mowgli was all alone in the wild, wide jungle. He kicked at the dust. He sat at the base of a rock and slumped over. He would never have admitted it, but he felt a little lonely without his friend.

Just then Mowgli heard someone singing. It was a dopey off-key sort of voice. Mowgli looked up. A big-bellied, scruffy-looking bear was dancing his way.

"Doo-be doo-be doo," sang the bear. He did a little soft-shoe and stopped short when he saw Mowgli.

"Well, now." He laughed good-naturedly. "What have we here?" He leaned over Mowgli and sniffed at him. Mowgli slapped the bear on the snout.

"OW!" said the bear.

"Go away!" shouted Mowgli. "Leave me alone."

The bear straightened himself up and peered down at the small boy. "That's pretty big talk, Little Britches," he said.

"I'm big enough," said Mowgli.

Mowgli punched the bear in the stomach, but the bear didn't even flinch. He just shook his head.

"Tsk, tsk, tsk," he said. "Pitiful. Hey, kid, you need help. Old Baloo's gonna teach you to fight like a bear."

Baloo shuffled his feet back and forth. He was quite a fighter and knew some fancy footwork. Mowgli watched Baloo's feet closely. He tried to imitate what the bear was doing.

"Yeah!" cried Baloo. "All right, kid! Now, loosen up. Get real loose and then start to weave a little. That's it! Now give me a big bear growl," Baloo instructed. "Scare me."

Mowgli growled. But he was just a little boy, and it was just a little growl.

"No!" cried Baloo. "I'm talking about like a *big* bear!"

To demonstrate, Baloo let out a growl that rumbled all the way up from the pit of his stomach and shook the trees as it rolled from his mouth.

A short ways away in the jungle, Bagheera heard the growl. When he'd stalked away, he hadn't gone very far. He was still worried about

Mowgli. He pricked up his ears and raced toward the sound.

"Oh, no!" he cried. "Mowgli's in trouble! I should never have left him alone!"

Bagheera was ready, once again, to rescue his little friend.

7

When Bagheera arrived at the river, what he saw surprised him. There was Baloo, hopping from one foot to the other, coaching Mowgli to fight like a bear.

"Oh, no!" Bagheera sighed. "It's Baloo, that shiftless, stupid jungle bum!"

"Keep moving," Baloo was shouting. "Weave about. That's it!"

Mowgli swung at Baloo. Baloo sidestepped him and then swung back. BAM! The big bear sent the little boy sprawling. Mowgli was knocked flat.

Bagheera shook his head in disgust.

"Fine teacher you are, old iron claws," he said. "Tell me, after you knock your pupil senseless, how do you expect him to remember the lesson?"

"Gee," Baloo said, surprised at his own strength. "I didn't mean to lay it on so hard."

Mowgli staggered to his feet.

"I'm a lot tougher than people think," he said dizzily.

Baloo grinned and started hopping around ready to play again.

"Let's go once more!" he said.

Mowgli swung at Baloo, and this time, Baloo fell backwards, as if he had been felled. Mowgli hopped on top of his furry friend and tickled him behind the ears.

"No!" Baloo laughed. "No! No tickling! We don't do that here in the jungle!"

Baloo pulled Mowgli onto his lap and ruffled the boy's hair.

"You're all right, kid," he said affectionately. "What do they call you?"

"Mowgli," answered Bagheera, who was still standing by, watching the hijinks. "And he's going to the Man-village. Right now!"

"Man-village?" said Baloo. "Why, they'll ruin him. They'll make a Man out of him!"

Mowgli hugged Baloo.

"Oh, Baloo," he cried. "I want to stay here with you!"

"Sure you do," said Baloo, hugging him back.

Bagheera raised his eyebrows.

"Oh?" he said. "And just how do you think he'll survive?"

"What do you mean?" Baloo said indignantly. "He's with me, isn't he? I'll teach him all I know."

"Well," Bagheera muttered under his breath, "that shouldn't take too long."

"Look, Little Britches, it's like this," said Baloo. Baloo put his arm around Mowgli and started to shuffle his feet again, doing his big bear dance. Baloo had some pretty particular ideas about life, and he made up a song to explain them to Mowgli. His ideas were very different from Bagheera's. Bagheera was strict, but Baloo was . . . well, Baloo was carefree. He didn't believe in worrying about anything.

"All you need in life are the bare necessities," he sang. "If you want food, all you have to do is pick it off the trees."

Mowgli reached for a prickly pear and pricked his finger on its spiny skin.

"OW!" he cried.

Baloo just chuckled. He pointed to some bees that were swarming around a flower. "See those bees?" he said. "You never want to work that hard. Relax. Remember: the bare necessities. That's all you need in life."

Mowgli laughed.

"You're lots of fun, Baloo," he said.

By this time, Baloo and Mowgli had danced quite a way down the bank and had left Bagheera far behind. Baloo slid lazily into the river.

"Oh, man," he sighed, "this is really living."

Mowgli nestled on top of Baloo's big, soft belly. "I like being a bear," said Mowgli.

"That's my boy," said Baloo. "You're going to make one swell bear."

The two drifted lazily down the river. Mowgli snuggled into Baloo's fur, lulled by the water's current. Neither of them noticed the band of monkeys that was swinging through the trees at the water's edge. Neither of them noticed the one monkey who reached down from the branch and grabbed Mowgli by the foot.

A fly buzzed by and landed on Baloo's nose.

"Hey, Mowgli," Baloo yawned, "how about flicking that mean old fly off your papa bear's nose?"

Something swiped hard at Baloo's snout. Baloo looked up. Why, that wasn't Mowgli lying on his belly. It was a monkey! Mowgli was gone! The monkeys had stolen him!

8

Baloo looked up. The trees above him were filled with chattering monkeys. The monkeys had Mowgli by the arm and were swinging him back and forth from one to another.

"Hey!" Mowgli was shouting. "Let go of me!"

"Take your flea-picking hands off my cub!" cried Baloo.

The monkeys knew they could tease the big bear.

"Come on and get him, champ!" they taunted.

Then, one monkey dangled Mowgli down the side of a tree. But when Baloo ran up to grab for him, the monkey yanked Mowgli quickly out of reach. Baloo banged right into the tree trunk and fell back, stunned. He raised himself and shook his fist at the monkeys.

"Give me back my Man-cub!" he shouted. The monkeys jumped up and down in the branches, chattering and laughing. One monkey picked a piece of fruit off the tree and threw it at Baloo.

SPLAT! It hit Baloo right in the nose.

"Look, monk," shouted Baloo. "You turn the Man-cub loose or I'll tie a knot in your tail!"

"We give up!" the monkeys laughed. "Here he comes! Catch!"

This time, when the monkeys swung Mowgli, they let him go and Mowgli went flying through the air.

"Baloo!" shouted the terrified Mowgli. "Catch me!"

Baloo backed up to try to catch his little friend. He didn't realize that he was backing up to the edge of a cliff.

"Back up!" the monkeys cheered him on. "Faster! Faster!"

Baloo reached up and was about to catch Mowgli when the monkeys grabbed the boy again and swung him out of reach. Then two monkeys skittered quickly to the edge of the cliff and stretched a vine across Baloo's path. When Baloo backed into it, he tripped and rolled down the side of the cliff into the deep ravine below.

"Baloo!" shouted Mowgli. "Help me! Baloo! They're carrying me away!"

As Baloo sat helpless at the bottom of the ravine, the wild monkeys carried off Mowgli. Baloo knew he needed help.

"Bagheera!" he shouted helplessly.

Bagheera was not far away when he heard Baloo's call. He got to the ravine just as Baloo was clawing his way up the steep face of the cliff.

"What happened?" asked Bagheera. "Where's Mowgli?"

"They ambushed me!" Baloo tried to explain. "Thousands of them. I jabbed with my left, then I swung with a right . . ."

Bagheera looked past Baloo, down into the ravine. Mowgli was nowhere in sight.

"For the last time," Bagheera snapped impatiently. "What happened to Mowgli?"

"Like I told you," said Baloo. "Them mangy monkeys carried him off."

Bagheera looked up through the thick leaves of the trees. There were no monkeys around anymore. He shook his head gravely.

"They must've taken him to the ancient ruins!" he said. "Oh, I hate to think what will happen when he meets that king of theirs."

9

The monkeys had, indeed, taken Mowgli to the ancient ruins, — an old, deserted temple that lay deep in the heart of the jungle. Their leader, King Louie, lived there. Louie was a big ape who ruled over all the monkeys.

When the monkeys got to the ruins, Louie was sitting on his throne with a banana peel on top of his head. He was just doing what he did best, monkeying around.

"We got him, King Louie!" the monkeys chattered. "Here he is! We got him! We got him!"

One monkey proudly held Mowgli up by the foot.

"Ha ha! So, you're the Man-cub!" said King Louie. "Crazy!"

Mowgli kicked to get free. "What do you want me for?" he demanded.

King Louie handed the boy a banana. "Word has reached my royal ear that you want to stay in the jungle," he said.

26

"Stay in the jungle?" Mowgli brightened. "I sure do!"

"Good. Old King Louie can fix that for you." Louie winked at Mowgli and handed him two more bananas. "Have we got a deal?"

"Yes, sir," said Mowgli. "I'll do anything to stay in the jungle."

"Well, then," said Louie, "I'll lay it on the line for you. I'm the king of the swingers, but I'm tired of monkeying around. I want to be a Man like you, Man-cub. I want to be human."

With that, Louie started dancing around. He was king of the swingers, all right. He started singing, too. Behind him, the monkeys gathered together as if they were a band, and each of them mimicked playing a musical instrument. It was a show! Mowgli had never seen anything quite like it. It was jazzy! It was hot! These monkeys had rhythm!

King Louie danced up to Mowgli and put his arm around the boy.

"Now, here's your part of the deal," said Louie. "Lay the secret on me of man's red fire."

"B-b-but I don't know how to make fire," Mowgli stuttered.

Louie grabbed Mowgli by the hair.

"Don't kid with me, Man-cub," he said gruffly. "I made a deal with you. I need Man's red fire to make my dream come true. Give me the secret."

Just outside the entrance to the ruins, two new pairs of eyes were watching the scene. It was Bagheera and Baloo. They had snuck up and were wondering how to rescue Mowgli.

"Fire!" said Bagheera when he heard King Louie's song. "So that's what that scoundrel's after!"

"I'll tear him limb from limb!" cried Baloo.

Baloo was angry, but he was having a hard time keeping quiet and standing still. All that jazzy music was getting inside him. He started to snap his fingers and move to the rhythm. Bagheera glared at Baloo, annoyed.

"Will you stop that silly beat business and listen," Bagheera snapped. "This is the plan. You create a disturbance and I'll rescue Mowgli."

Baloo started tapping his feet. Before Bagheera could stop him, he was dancing full out, carried away by the music.

"Yeah!" he said, as if in a trance. "Create a disturbance. I'm gone, man!"

Baloo started dancing through the entrance to the ruins.

"Not yet, Baloo!" Bagheera cried.

But it was too late. Baloo was gone. And King Louie and the monkeys had formed a dance line. They were snaking right toward Bagheera!

10

As King Louie and the line of dancing monkeys rounded the corner, Bagheera looked around frantically for a place to hide. As luck would have it, there was a marble statue of a panther guarding the entrance door. Bagheera jumped next to the statue and quickly assumed the same pose, so that he looked like a statue, too. The monkeys danced right by him without even noticing.

At the end of the dance line was Mowgli. Bagheera reached out his paw to grab for the boy. But before he could reach him, a door swung open and knocked him back. It was Baloo! Baloo was dressed as a girl! He had a grass skirt slung around his heavy hips and had set a leafy plant on top of his head to look like hair. Over his snout he wore two coconut halves. Baloo looked like a female ape!

Baloo danced out in time to the music. He swiveled his hips flirtatiously. King Louie ran right over to dance with Baloo. The ape king was enchanted! He had never seen such a beautiful ape. And, boy, could she dance!

King Louie grabbed Baloo's hand and started to do a fast jitterbug dance. Baloo and King Louie were rocking and rolling. The monkeys went wild. Everybody started dancing. Everybody was having a good time.

Baloo batted his eyelashes coyly at King Louie. King Louie smiled back. The king was in love. He reached over and gave Baloo an affectionate love tap on the behind. But that put an end to the romance. The love pat was a little more powerful than he expected. It knocked the plant off Baloo's head and the coconuts off his snout. King Louie blinked his eyes, confused. What had happened to his beautiful new girlfriend?

"It's Baloo, the bear!" shouted one of the monkeys.

"Yeah, that's him!" shouted another. "How'd that square get in here?"

Mowgli ran up to hug his friend.

"Baloo, it's you!" he cried.

Baloo caught him up and started running. But just then, one of the monkeys swooped down, grabbed Mowgli right out of Baloo's hands and ran the other way. The chase was on!

Everybody got in on the chase. Baloo raced after the monkeys. Bagheera was not far behind.

Then King Louie grabbed Mowgli's hand and

pulled the boy behind him. Baloo grabbed Mowgli's other hand. The three of them whipped around an old stone pillar that was holding up the edge of the ruins and the pillar gave way under the weight. The temple had no support! It started to crumble!

King Louie dropped Mowgli and ran to hold up the falling stones. He tried to support the building, but he just couldn't hold up all that weight. All around him, stones were falling. The ancient temple was collapsing!

Baloo, Mowgli, and Bagheera ran from the falling debris as fast as they could. When they got to a nearby hill, they stopped and looked back at the temple. It was completely in shambles. The stones had knocked King Louie and all his monkeys senseless.

Baloo broke out into a big, wide grin.

"Man," he laughed, "that's what I call a swinging party!"

11

Baloo and Bagheera had successfully rescued Mowgli from the ape king, but Bagheera was still worried. Late that night, while Mowgli slept soundly in a bed of leaves, the panther sat up talking to the bear.

"And furthermore, Baloo," he was saying, "Mowgli seems to have Man's ability to get into trouble. And your influence hasn't been exactly — "

"Shhh!" Baloo cut him off. "Keep it down. You're going to wake the little buddy." Baloo walked over to Mowgli and covered the boy with a blanket of leaves. "He's had a long day," he said. "You know, it ain't easy learning to be like me."

Bagheera frowned.

"Baloo," he said firmly. "The Man-cub must go to the Man-village. The jungle is not the place for him."

Baloo just shrugged. "I grew up in the jungle," he said. "Take a look at me."

Bagheera took a frank look at the bear. Baloo was scratched and bruised from the fight he had had that night at the ancient ruins.

"Yes," Bagheera said. "Just look at yourself. Baloo, you can't adopt Mowgli as your son."

"Why not?" said Baloo.

"Because birds of a feather should flock together," Bagheera tried to explain.

"Oh, stop worrying, Baggy," said Baloo. "I'll take care of him."

Bagheera looked straight at Baloo.

"Yes," he said. "Like you did when the monkeys kidnapped him, huh?"

"Can't a guy make one mistake?" Baloo shrugged.

"Not in the jungle!" said Bagheera. "Listen, sooner or later, Mowgli will meet Shere Khan."

"The tiger?" Baloo winced. "What's he got against the kid?"

"He hates Man, with a vengeance!" Bagheera exclaimed. "You know that! He fears Man's gun and Man's fire."

"But little Mowgli doesn't have those things," said Baloo.

"Shere Khan won't wait until he does," said Bagheera. "He'll get Mowgli while he's young and helpless."

"No!" cried Baloo. "We can't let that happen! What are we going to do? You name it, I'll do it."

"Good," said Bagheera. "Then make Mowgli go to the Man-village. It's up to you."

Baloo loved Mowgli. The last thing in the world he wanted was to give the boy up. But, in his heart, he knew he had to do what was best for the boy. And he knew that Bagheera was probably right.

The morning sun was just beginning to rise over the steamy jungle. Baloo looked down at Mowgli. He knelt at the boy's side and tapped him gently on the shoulder.

"Mowgli," he said. "It's time to get up."

Mowgli opened his eyes and smiled a sleepy smile when he saw his friend Baloo.

"Rub that old sleep out of your eyes," said Baloo. "You and me, we got a long walk ahead of us."

"Swell," said Mowgli. Without asking any questions, he jumped to his feet and took Baloo's hand in his. He was always happy to go with Baloo.

"Good-bye, Bagheera!" he called over his shoulder. "Me and Baloo, we've got things to do!"

Bagheera watched the two walk off into the jungle.

"Good-bye, Man-cub," he said. He knew this might be the last time he would ever lay eyes on the boy. "Good luck!" he called after him.

Mowgli skipped ahead on the path. Baloo padded sadly behind him.

"All we need are the bare necessities," Mowgli said brightly, repeating the very lesson that Baloo had taught him. Mowgli grabbed two bananas from a tree. He popped one in his mouth and tossed the other to Baloo.

"I like being a bear," said Mowgli. "I'll live here in the jungle all my life."

"Look, buddy," said Baloo. "There's something I've got to tell you." Baloo took a deep breath. He didn't know how to tell the boy the truth. "Mowgli," he said. "Don't you realize that you're a human?"

"I'm not, anymore," said Mowgli. "I'm a bear, just like you!"

Mowgli swiped playfully at Baloo, fighting just the way Baloo had taught him. Baloo grabbed Mowgli's hands in his.

"Little buddy, listen to me!" Baloo pleaded. "I'm trying to tell you something important."

Mowgli looked up at Baloo questioningly. Baloo swallowed hard, then blurted out the news.

"I've got to take you to the Man-village," he said.

Mowgli's eyes narrowed. He yanked his hands from Baloo's.

"The Man-village!" he cried angrily. "But you said we were partners." Mowgli backed away, pointing his finger at Baloo. "Why, you're . . . you're just like old Bagheera!" he cried.

And before Baloo could stop him, Mowgli turned and ran off alone into the jungle.

"Wait!" Baloo cried after him. "Stop! Mowgli! Mowgli!"

Once again, Bagheera heard Baloo's cries. When he bounded through the brush and found Baloo standing alone, he figured out exactly what had happened.

"Well, don't just stand there!" he cried. "Let's separate. We've got to find him!"

Bagheera sprinted in one direction and Baloo lumbered off in another.

"If anything happens to that little fellow, I'll never forgive myself," said Baloo. He parted the bushes and scanned the jungle beyond. "Mowgli!" he cried desperately. "Mowgli!"

12

Bagheera and Baloo had good reason to be worried about Mowgli. Shere Khan, the ferocious tiger, was prowling nearby, stalking the brush, looking for prey. The tiger had not yet come upon Mowgli. He was crouched behind some ferns, eyeing a sweet gazelle who was drinking from a clear, cool pond. Just as he was ready to pounce, a loud trumpet sounded behind him. It was the elephant Dawn Patrol! They were marching right past the pond. Shere Khan ducked for cover.

"What beastly luck!" he muttered. "Confound that ridiculous Colonel Hathi."

Shere Khan was not the only one who heard the patrol's approach. Bagheera did, too. And he needed the elephants' help. Bagheera leaped through the branches of the trees to stop them.

"HALT!" Bagheera cried as the elephants marched past. The patrol stopped short. Colonel Hathi looked up angrily.

"Who said 'halt'?" he bellowed. "*I* give the commands around here."

"It was me, Colonel," said Bagheera, coming forward on the branch. "I'm sorry, but I need your help."

"Absolutely impossible," said Colonel Hathi. "We're on a cross-country march."

"But it's an emergency, Colonel," Bagheera explained. "The Man-cub must be found."

"Man-cub?" Colonel Hathi looked puzzled. "What Man-cub?"

"The one I was taking to the Man-village," said Bagheera.

"Good," said Colonel Hathi. "That's where he belongs."

"But he ran away," Bagheera continued. "And Shere Khan is sure to pick up the Man-cub's trail."

"Shere Khan?" the Colonel snorted. "Nonsense, old boy. Shere Khan isn't within miles of here."

Of course, that was not true. Shere Khan was just beyond, hiding in the bushes. And he was listening to every word they said.

"I'm sorry, Bagheera," Colonel Hathi continued. "I just can't help you. Fortunes of war and all that."

Colonel Hathi turned to go. But his wife, her baby in tow, broke ranks from the patrol and stepped directly in front of him, blocking his way.

"This has gone far enough," she said. "How

would you like to have *our* boy lost and alone in the jungle? You help find the Man-cub or I'm taking over command."

"That's preposterous!" said Colonel Hathi.

"Pop," the baby elephant said, tugging at his father's leg, "the Man-cub and I are friends. He'll get hurt if we don't find him."

Colonel Hathi looked down at his son. The baby looked so young. And the jungle was so dangerous. . . .

"Don't you worry, son," said the Colonel. He was softening. "Your father had a plan in mind all the time."

The Colonel faced his troops and cleared his throat.

"The company will move out on a new mission," he said. "We will find the lost Man-cub."

"Oh, thank you, Colonel," said Bagheera. "There's no time to lose."

The elephants fell into line and marched ahead, crashing through the brush. Bagheera brought up the rear.

From his hiding place in the brush, Shere Khan watched them march off. He licked his chops. "And now for my rendezvous with the little lost Man-cub!" he growled.

13

Everyone was looking for Mowgli, but he was not far away. He was wandering through the brush by himself, feeling a little lonely. He picked up a rock and skipped it across the surface of the river. Then he sat down at the base of a large tree and buried his head in his hands.

As it happened, Kaa, the big python, was sitting up in a branch of that tree. When Kaa saw Mowgli, he lowered his tail, scooped the boy up and lifted him up into the branches.

"Kaa! It's you!" said Mowgli.

"Yes-s-s, Man-cub," Kaa hissed. "S-s-so nice to s-s-see you again."

Mowgli tried to free himself from Kaa's tail. He turned his head to avoid Kaa's hypnotic gaze.

"You don't want me to look at you?" said Kaa. "Then you can look at me."

"No, sir!" said Mowgli. "I know what you're trying to do."

"Oh, you do?" said Kaa. "You don't trust me?"

"No!" said Mowgli. He covered his eyes with his arm.

"Well," Kaa said, backing away, "then there's nothing I can do to help you."

"Help me?" Mowgli uncovered his eyes. "You want to help me?"

"Certainly." Kaa smiled. "I can see to it that you never leave this jungle."

"How could you do that?" asked Mowgli.

Kaa's smile turned into a hungry leer.

"Oh, I have my ways," he said. Kaa sidled up to Mowgli and tried again to catch his eye. "But first," he said, "you must trust me."

"I don't trust anyone anymore," said Mowgli.

Kaa slid down in front of the boy and stared directly into his eyes.

"I'm not like those fair-weather friends of yours," he said. "You can trust me. Trust me."

Mowgli was transfixed. He began to be lulled by Kaa's chant. "Trust me. Sleep. Slumber." Mowgli's eyes rolled back. He had again been hypnotized.

Kaa coiled himself around the boy and licked his lips. He opened his mouth wide. The sleeping boy would make a tasty dinner. But just as Kaa was about to swallow Mowgli, someone pulled on his tail.

"Oh, now what?" Kaa said irritatedly. "Who is it?"

"It's me, Shere Khan," came a voice. It was the tiger! Kaa knew he had to hide his prey.

"Shere Khan! What a surprise!" said Kaa. He covered Mowgli with his coils and dropped his head down from the limb to greet Shere Khan.

"Forgive me if I've interrupted anything," said Shere Khan. He stared up into the branches of the tree.

"No, no," Kaa smiled. "Nothing at all."

"Ah," said Khan. "I thought you were entertaining someone. I thought I heard you singing to someone."

"Just singing to myself," Kaa said, trying to look innocent.

"I'm searching for a Man-cub," Shere Khan went on. "The one who's lost." He looked suspiciously up at the tree. "Now, where do you suppose he could be?"

"Search me," shrugged Kaa.

"That's an excellent idea," said Shere Khan. "I'm sure you wouldn't mind showing me your coils."

Kaa dropped his tail down to show that it was empty. Then he carefully unwound his middle coils from around Mowgli and dropped them down to show them, too.

Shere Khan stared up into the tree. He wasn't sure if he believed Kaa.

"Hmm," said Shere Khan. "Well, if you do just

happen to see the Man-cub, you will inform me first. Understand?"

He brought his paw up to Kaa's face and bared his claws threateningly.

"I get the point," gulped Kaa.

"Good show," said Shere Khan. "Now I must continue my search for the helpless little lad."

And then, with one last glance back up at the tree, Shere Khan turned and slunk back through the jungle.

Up in the tree, the "helpless little lad" had just awakened. He hoisted himself out of Kaa's coils and then reached over and pushed the snake off the branch.

"Aaaagh!" cried Kaa as he fell to the ground.

Mowgli jumped down from the tree.

"You told me a lie, Kaa!" he said. "You said I could trust you."

"It's like you said," said Kaa. "You can't trust anyone."

Mowgli backed away from Kaa. Kaa started to slither toward him, but, in the fall, Kaa's tail had knotted. It stuck between two small trees and held him back.

Mowgli was safe! He ran from the snake, back into the thick jungle. Once again he had escaped!

14

In a nearby part of the jungle, four vultures were sitting on a branch of an old, burned-out tree. All the land around them was dry and parched. The vultures' names were Flaps, Dizzy, Buzzie, and Ziggy. There wasn't an awful lot of life in their part of the jungle. The vultures were bored and looking for something to do.

Buzzie leaned idly against the tree. "What are we going to do?" he asked.

"I don't know," said Flaps. "What do *you* want to do?"

Flaps looked out across the land. In the distance, he spotted a boy walking toward them. The boy's head was hanging low. His shoulders were hunched and he was kicking up stones in his path.

"Hey, what in the world is that?" said Flaps.

It was Mowgli.

"Come on, lads!" said Ziggy. "Let's have some fun with this little bloke."

The vultures flew off the tree and swooped down around Mowgli.

44

"Blimey," said Flaps, poking fun. "He's got legs like a stork, he has."

"Like a stork, he has," agreed Buzzie, "but he ain't got no feathers, he ain't."

Mowgli looked up at the vultures, but didn't say a word. He simply turned and walked the other way, across the burned-out landscape.

"What's wrong with him?" asked Dizzy.

"I think we overdid it," said Flaps.

"Aw," said Buzzie softly, "just look at him." Mowgli did, indeed, look a sorry sight. "Why, the poor little fellow. He must be down on his luck."

The vultures flapped to catch up with Mowgli.

"Hey! Wait a minute, kid!" they called. "What's wrong? You look like you haven't got a friend in the world."

"I haven't," said Mowgli sadly. "Nobody wants me around."

Buzzie put his wing around Mowgli's shoulder to comfort him.

"Kid," he said, "we're going to let you join our group. We're going to make you an honorary vulture. Everybody's got to have friends."

Buzzie beckoned his three friends. Then he waved his wing like a conductor, and the vultures burst into song. They sang a song about friendship. Little by little, Mowgli began to cheer up. A smile broke across his face. Soon he was singing along with them.

Everyone was having fun. They didn't notice that another animal had slipped through the grass and was watching them. The intruder was Shere Khan. When the song was over, Shere Khan burst into applause.

"Bravo! Bravo!" he cried. "An extraordinary performance!"

At the sight of the vicious tiger, the vultures all backed away. Mowgli, though, stood fast. Above them, the sky darkened and a crack of thunder rumbled in the air. The tiger smiled and started walking toward Mowgli.

"And thank you for detaining my victim," he leered.

"Let's get out of here!" cried Dizzy.

Buzzie knocked Dizzy back as he, too, tried to scramble to safety. "Gang way!" he cried.

The vultures flew up to their tree branch, out of the tiger's reach.

"Run!" they called back to Mowgli. "Run, friend! Run!"

15

All the animals in the jungle feared Shere Khan. But not Mowgli. The vultures in the tree were shouting at Mowgli to run, but he stood firm. He folded his arms across his chest and faced the tiger.

"Run?" he said. "Why should I run?"

Shere Khan bared his claws threateningly.

"Why should you run?" he said. "Could it be possible that you don't know who I am?"

"I know who you are, all right," said Mowgli. "You're Shere Khan. You don't scare me. I won't run from anyone."

Shere Khan stared at Mowgli. He had never before met anyone who wasn't afraid of him.

"Ah," he said slowly. "You have spirit for one so small, and such spirit is deserving of a sporting chance." Shere Khan leaned his head against a nearby tree and covered his eyes, as if he were going to play hide-and-seek. "Now," he said, "I'm going to close my eyes and count to ten. It makes the chase more interesting."

Shere Khan began his count. "One, two, three." Mowgli did not move. "Four, five, six." Mowgli picked a large stick off the ground and raised it high to defend himself. "Seven, eight, nine, . . . TEN!"

The tiger turned and sprang for Mowgli.

"RRRROWRRR!" he cried.

But, just as his claws were about to tear into the boy's flesh, he was pulled up short. Somone had caught him by the tail. It was Baloo! Baloo was using all his strength to hold the tiger back.

"Run, Mowgli! Run!" yelled Baloo.

"Let go, you big oaf!" shouted Shere Khan.

Shere Khan swiped at Baloo and tugged at his tail to try to free it, but Baloo held fast. Shere Khan circled around to reach for Baloo from behind. He bit Baloo on the tail.

"YEEOW!" cried Baloo.

Just when it seemed as if the tiger might win, Mowgli ran up with his stick and clobbered Shere Khan on the nose. The tiger roared. He took off after Mowgli, with Baloo still holding tightly to his tail.

"Somebody do something with that kid!" shouted Baloo.

"Come on, lads!" cried Buzzie.

Shere Khan was gaining on Mowgli. He reached

out his paw and tried to lunge at the boy.

SWOOP! Just in time, the vultures swept down, grabbed Mowgli in their talons, and lifted him out of the tiger's reach. They carried him to the safety of the tree.

"Let go!" cried Mowgli. "Baloo needs help!"

Mowgli was safe, but Baloo did not let go of Shere Khan's tail. The tiger was angry. He turned to attack Baloo.

Another clap of thunder pierced the air. Black clouds gathered, threatening a violent storm. Shere Khan rammed Baloo into a tree and knocked the bear flat. Baloo tried to get to his feet, but he fell back dizzily.

"I'll kill you for this," Shere Khan said slowly. The tiger advanced for the kill.

Suddenly a bolt of lightning shot down from the sky and hit the tree where the vultures were holding Mowgli. The tree burst into flames.

"Fire!" cried Buzzie. The vultures and Mowgli jumped to safety. Buzzie looked back at the burning tree. That gave him an idea. "Fire is the only thing old stripes is afraid of!" he said.

Mowgli ran toward the burning tree.

"Go!" Flaps called after him. "You get the fire, and we'll do the rest!"

16

Shere Khan's eyes gleamed as he walked toward poor Baloo. He knocked Baloo down a second time. Baloo was too hurt to even try to fight back. Shere Khan hit Baloo in the stomach. He punched him in the face. Then, with a vicious laugh, he delivered one final, crushing blow. Baloo was knocked senseless. The tiger had won.

"Charge!"

Shere Khan didn't have much time to enjoy his victory. The vultures swooped down on him, attacking him from the air. Shere Khan bared his claws and reared up at them.

"Stay out of this, you mangy fools!" he cried.

Shere Khan swiped at the vultures, but they flapped their wings, hovering just out of reach.

"Missed me by a mile, he did!" laughed Buzzie.

Flaps flew down and pulled at Shere Khan's whiskers.

"He's a bloomin' pussycat, he is!" teased Flaps.

While the vultures were distracting Shere Khan, Mowgli crept up on the tiger from behind. Mowgli had picked up a flaming branch that had fallen from the burning tree. He lifted Shere Khan's tail and quickly tied the branch to it.

"Look behind you, chum!" taunted Dizzy.

Shere Khan spun around and saw the flaming branch. Fire!

"YEOW!" yelled Shere Khan.

He jumped into the air to try to escape it, but the branch was tied fast. The flames licked at him and singed his fur. As he lashed his tail to try to get free, the flames leaped higher. Shere Khan took off running. The vultures laughed as they watched the tiger retreat and disappear over the crest of the hill, pursued by his worst enemy, fire.

"Well, that's the last of him," said Buzzie.

"Took off like a flamin' comet, he did," said Flaps.

"Come on," said Buzzie. "Let's go congratulate our friend."

A few feet away, Mowgli was kneeling at Baloo's side. A soft rain had begun to fall.

"Hold it, fellows," said Dizzy, as the vultures walked toward them. "Now's not the time for congratulations. Look."

Baloo's eyes were closed and Mowgli was cradling Baloo's head in his arms. The bear's big, mangy body lay in a still, lifeless heap.

"Baloo!" Mowgli was crying. "Baloo, get up. Oh, please, get up."

Tears smarted Mowgli's eyes. He grabbed Baloo by the shoulders and shook him. But Baloo did not move.

17

As Mowgli leaned over and hugged the bear's heavy head to his own, Bagheera arrived. Bagheera saw what had happened and walked slowly over to comfort Mowgli. The poor boy had had a lot of upheaval in his young life.

"Mowgli," Bagheera said softly. "Try to understand."

"But what's the matter with him?" Mowgli asked, his eyes wide, not understanding.

Bagheera lowered his head in grief.

"You've got to be brave like Baloo was," he said simply.

Mowgli stared straight into Bagheera's eyes.

"You don't mean . . ." he said. "Oh, no!" he wailed. "Baloo!"

His friend was dead! Mowgli collapsed in sobs.

As the rain poured down around them, Bagheera put his paw on Mowgli's shoulder, then stepped back to say a few words about his dear, departed friend.

"Now, now," he said. "I know how you feel. But try to think of it this way. When great deeds are remembered in this jungle, one name will stand above all others — our friend, Baloo the Bear."

Mowgli was sobbing. The vultures were crying, too. Everyone was so busy crying that no one noticed Baloo. Baloo cracked one eye open. He wasn't dead at all! He had simply been in a daze, and now he was coming to.

Bagheera went on with his graveside speech. His voice rang through the jungle.

"The memory of Baloo's sacrifice and bravery will forever be engraved on our saddened hearts," he said.

Baloo started sniffling. They were talking about him!

"This spot where Baloo fell will always be a hallowed place in the jungle," Bagheera said. "For here lies one of nature's noblest creatures."

"Beautiful," Baloo sniffed quietly.

Bagheera patted Mowgli on the back.

"It's best we leave now," he said. "Come on, Man-cub."

"Hey!" Baloo called after them. He lifted his head off the ground. "Don't stop now, Baggy. You're doin' great. There's more! There's more!"

At the sound of Baloo's voice, Bagheera spun around. He was shocked to see the bear's big, wet face grinning up at him. Baloo was alive!

"Why, you big fraud!" Bagheera yelled at him.

Mowgli ran up to Baloo and threw his arms around the bear's neck.

"Baloo!" he cried. "You're all right!"

"Who, me?" Baloo laughed. "I sure am. I never felt better."

The sun had come back out and was peeking through the clouds. Baloo staggered to his feet and steadied himself on the muddy ground.

"I was just takin' five," he chuckled, "playin' it cool."

Baloo scooped Mowgli up in his arms and hoisted the boy onto his shoulders. The vultures watched as Baloo turned and carried Mowgli back into the thick of the jungle. Bagheera was still in shock. He padded slowly after them, not knowing what to say.

Dizzy shook his head.

"It's going to be a bit dull without the little bloke, isn't it?" he said.

"So what are we going to do?" asked Buzzie.

"I don't know. What do you want to do?" Flaps answered.

The vultures groaned.

"Hey, don't start that again!" said Flaps.

The vultures perched on their branch. Once again, they had plenty of time, but nothing to do. They were right back where they started.

18

Baloo danced down the path, with Mowgli still on his shoulders.

"Hey, Baggy," he called back to Bagheera, "too bad you missed the action. You should've seen how I made a sucker out of old stripes. BOOM! I hit him with a left hook to the jaw."

Bagheera rolled his eyes. He knew Baloo was bragging. He didn't even bother to argue.

Baloo gave Mowgli an affectionate chuck under the chin.

"You want to know something?" he said to his young friend. "We're good sparring partners."

"You'd better believe it!" said Mowgli.

Baloo lifted Mowgli off his shoulders and gave him a big bear hug.

"Yes, sir," said Baloo. "Nothing or nobody is ever going to come between us again."

The three friends walked down the path. Baloo didn't realize it, but they were nearing the Man-village. The sound of someone singing drifted toward them. Mowgli slid out of Baloo's arms and ran toward the sound. He parted the bushes and peered through. A young girl was walking toward them. She was carrying a large water jug on her head.

"Look!" whispered Mowgli. "What's that?"

"That's the Man-village," said Bagheera.

"No, no! I mean *that!*" said Mowgli. He pointed right at the girl. She had stopped at the stream and was dipping her water jug into the clear, cool water.

"Forget about those," Baloo advised Mowgli. "They're nothin' but trouble."

Mowgli's eyes were fixed on the girl. She was humming while she worked. Mowgli thought she looked pretty.

"I've never seen one before," said Mowgli.

"So, you've seen one," said Baloo. "Now, let's go."

"Just a minute," said Mowgli. "I'll be right back. I want a better look."

Mowgli scampered away from his friends and hoisted himself up onto a branch of a nearby tree to get a better look. Baloo watched him worriedly. Bagheera smiled. He knew that Mowgli belonged in the Man-village, that he'd be happier with his own kind.

As Mowgli climbed out to the end of the tree branch, a leaf loosened and fluttered down into the stream below. The girl looked up. When she noticed Mowgli, she looked into his eyes and smiled directly at him. Mowgli was so surprised, he slipped and fell off the branch. SPLASH! He landed in the water. Mowgli's cheeks burned with embarrassment. He scrambled out of the water and hid behind the bushes at the side of the stream.

While Mowgli watched from behind the bushes, the girl filled her jug with water and set it back on top of her head. She started walking slowly back up the path, singing as she went. Mowgli was spellbound. He couldn't keep his eyes off her. He had never heard such a beautiful song or seen such a beautiful creature.

The girl knew Mowgli was watching her. She glanced back at him and smiled flirtatiously. Then, she tipped the jug off her head so that it fell and rolled down the dirt path to Mowgli's feet.

Baloo, who was watching the whole scene, couldn't believe his eyes.

"She did that on purpose!" he said angrily.

Bagheera laughed.

"Obviously," he replied.

The two watched as Mowgli grabbed up the jug and filled it with water at the stream. Then Mowgli set the jug on his own head and hurried up the path after the girl.

"Mowgli, come back!" cried Baloo.

But Mowgli was gone. The girl had lured him into the Man-village. After all the years of living in the wild, Mowgli had finally gone back to his own kind.

"He's hooked," Baloo sighed, as he watched his friend go off.

"It was bound to happen," said Bagheera. "Mowgli is where he belongs now."

"Yeah. I guess you're right," said Baloo. "But I still think he'd make one swell bear."

Baloo put his arm around Bagheera. He was too carefree a soul to dwell very long on anything that was sad.

"Well, come on, Baggy, buddy," he said. "Let's go back to where we belong."

Baloo and Bagheera turned and headed back into the thick, wild jungle. As they were walking, Baloo started dancing.

"Hey, get with the beat, Baggy," he called back to his friend. The sun streamed down on them through the lush jungle leaves. The jungle was their home. Who knew what adventure it would bring next?